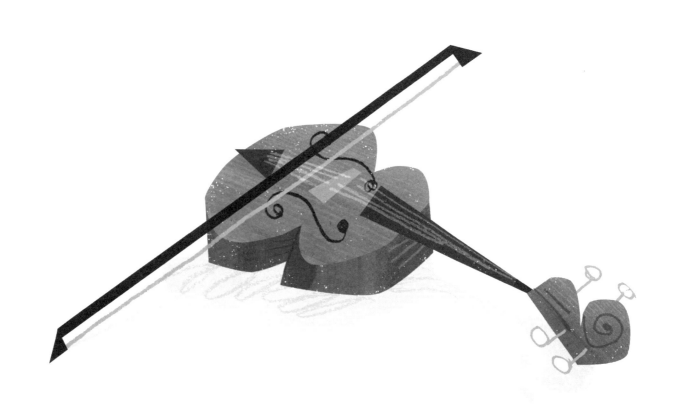

To Mr and Mrs Jack & Lucy Gray! K.G.
For Bonnie and Sonny F.B.

HODDER CHILDREN'S BOOKS
First published in Great Britain in 2020 by Hodder and Stoughton

A CIP catalogue record for this book is available from the British Library.

HB ISBN: 978 1 444 95367 1
PB ISBN: 978 1 444 95368 8

1 3 5 7 9 10 8 6 4 2

Printed and bound in China

Hodder Children's Books
An imprint of Hachette Children's Group
Part of Hodder and Stoughton
Carmelite House, 50 Victoria Embankment
London, EC4Y 0DZ

An Hachette UK Company
www.hachette.co.uk
www.hachettechildrens.co.uk

www.kesgray.com
www.fredbluntillustration.com

THE DIDDLE THAT DUMMED

KES GRAY AND
FRED BLUNT

Flinty Bo Diddle
was writing a tune for his fiddle.

And it was going very, very well . . .

"STOP!"

shouted Flinty,
halfway through
the tune.

"Who did a dum?
Who did a **DUM?**
You were
meant to do a
DIDDLE
not a
DUM!"

"**Sorry,**"
said the diddle that dummed.
"I'm **not** like other diddles.

Sometimes I like to go dum."

"Go dum?" frowned Flinty. "GO DUM!
You can't go dum. You're a diddle not a dum.
I put you in the middle to go diddle, not DUM!"

"Let's try again,"
said the diddle that dummed.

"Did I?"
said the diddle that dummed.

"Yes, you definitely did," said all the other diddles. "It was just as we got to the middle. Instead of going diddle you definitely went dum."

"Won't a dum do?"
asked the diddle that dummed.

"OF COURSE A DUM WON'T DO!"

shouted Flinty.

"The tune for my fiddle is a tune full of **diddles**, diddles that go

diddle, diddle, diddle, diddle

all the way to the end!"

"Try me at the **beginning**," said the diddle that dummed. "If you put me at the beginning instead of in the middle, maybe I'll remember to go diddle."

Flinty rearranged his diddles and tried again . . .

"YOU DID IT AGAIN!"

growled Flinty, shaking his fiddle.

"Try me at the end," said the diddle that dummed.

"YOU DID IT AGAIN!"

hollered Flinty, jumping on his fiddle.

"Sorry," said the diddle that dummed.
"Maybe we should change the tune?"

"Change the tune?" said Flinty.
"What do you mean, change the tune?"

"I mean maybe, instead of us all going
diddle, perhaps we could all go dum?"

Flinty thought long and hard.

"Do you know, it might just work!" he said, "but it will never be a tune for my fiddle. It will have to be a tune for my **drum.**"

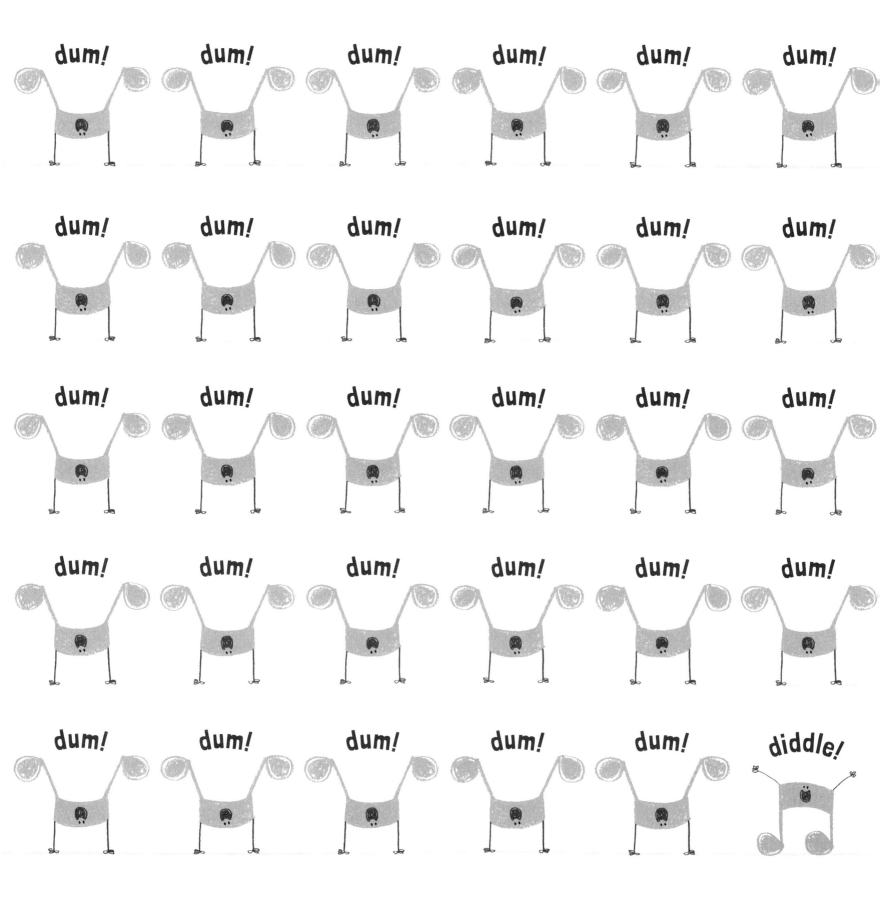

"NOW LOOK WHAT YOU DID!"
raged Flinty.
"NOW INSTEAD OF GOING
DUM YOU WENT DIDDLE!"

"**Sorry,**"
said the diddle that dummed,
but now diddled.
"I'm not very good at this, am I?

Please can I go to the loo?"

"Yes, please can we go the loo too?"
asked the diddles that diddled but now dummed.

"If you **must**," sighed Flinty,
"if you **must**."

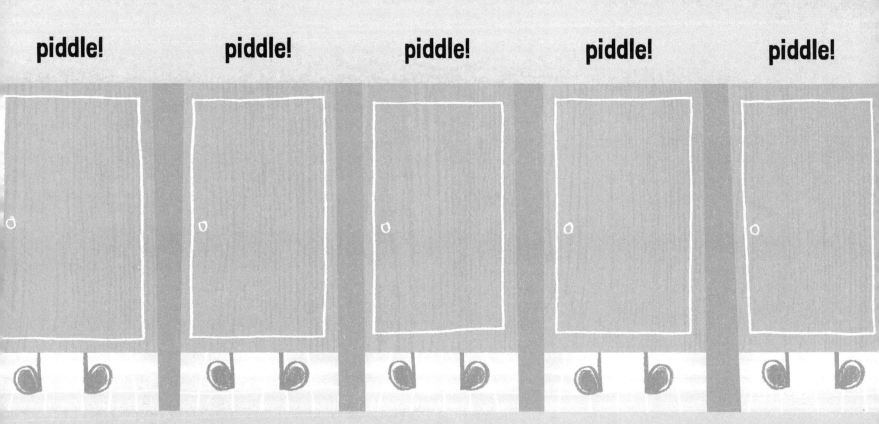

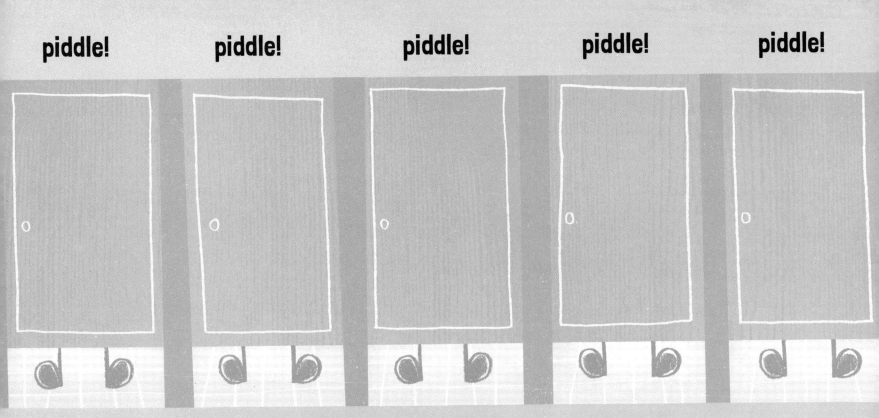

plop!